Evelyn
the Mermicorn
Fairy

For Coco, who loves mermicorns
and always speaks her mind

Special thanks to
Rachel Elliot

ISBN 978-1-338-55384-0

10 9 8 7 6 5 4 3 2 1   19 20 21 22 23

Printed in the U.S.A.   40
First printing 2019

Evelyn
the Mermicorn
Fairy

by Daisy Meadows

Scholastic Inc.

Now Topaz makes each fairy pest
Quite confident that they know best.
But when I steal her gems so bright,
Each fairy's wisdom will take flight.

I'll make them fear and hesitate,
Until they're in an awful state.
And when they cannot give advice,
I'll cover Fairyland in ice!

Find the hidden letters in the stars throughout this book. Unscramble all ten letters to spell a special mermicorn word!

Believing in Yourself

Contents

A Rainy Morning
in Tippington

"I love listening to the rain beating
on the window," said Rachel Walker.
"Especially when it's so cozy inside."
She snuggled deeper into her favorite
armchair and gazed into the flickering

flames of the fire. Her best friend, Kirsty
Tate, put down the pattern she was
stitching.

"Me, too," she said.

Kirsty was spending the last week
of the holidays at Rachel's house in
Tippington. Although they went to
different schools, they saw each other as
often as they could. They always had fun
when they were together, and they often
shared secret, magical adventures with
their fairy friends.

The living room door opened and
Rachel's dad popped his head around it.

"Anyone for hot chocolate?" he asked.

"Yes please," said the girls together.

"With whipped cream and sprinkles?"
Rachel added.

"Of course," said Mr. Walker. "Maybe

it'll make up for not being able to go pebble collecting on the beach. What did you want the pebbles for?"

"We were going to paint inspiring pictures and messages on them, and then put them back on the beach for other people to find," Rachel explained.

"But it's OK," said Kirsty. "We found something else crafty to do instead."

Rachel's dad looked at the cross-stitch patterns they were holding. Kirsty was working on a turquoise mermaid with golden hair, and Rachel was stitching a snow-white unicorn.

"Those look complicated," he said.

"Yes, but it'll be a great feeling when they're finished," said Kirsty.

Mr. Walker went to make the hot chocolate, and the girls continued stitching.

"What's your favorite, mermaids or unicorns?" asked Rachel.

"I don't think I can choose," said Kirsty. "After all, we've met them both on our adventures, and each one was just as magical and inspiring as the other."

Just then, they heard a tiny, tinkling giggle. The girls exchanged a surprised glance.

"That sounded exactly like a fairy," said Rachel.

There was another bell-like giggle, and the girls jumped to their feet.

"Where are you?" Kirsty asked.

Then Rachel noticed that Kirsty's dark

hair was sprinkled with
sparkling fairy dust. Kirsty
saw the same thing on
Rachel's hair. They both
looked up at the same
time and laughed out
loud.

A chestnut-haired
fairy was waving at
them from the top

of the round glass light pendant. She slid down it with a whoop and turned somersaults through the air, landing on the sofa arm with a bounce. She was wearing a shimmering, glittery blue skirt and a matching denim jacket.

"Hello," she said. "I'm Evelyn the Mermicorn Fairy."

"Hello, Evelyn," said Rachel, kneeling down in front of her. "What brings you to my living room?"

"And what's a mermicorn?" Kirsty added.

"Exactly what it sounds like," said

Evelyn with a smile. "It's the rarest, most magical creature in all of Fairyland— half-mermaid and half-unicorn."

"Oh, it sounds wonderful," said Kirsty in a whisper. "I wish I could see one."

"We only see them once a year," said Evelyn. "We always celebrate their visit with the Mermicorn Festival. That's why

I'm here. Would you like to come and enjoy the festival with me?"

Rachel and Kirsty squealed in excitement.

"We'd love to," said Kirsty.

"Then it's time to go to Fairyland!" said Evelyn.

A Fairy Without a Wand

Evelyn opened her hand, and the girls saw that she was holding a little pile of sparkling fairy dust.

"Don't you have a wand?" asked Rachel.

Evelyn smiled.

"Not today," she said.

She blew the fairy dust toward the girls, and a pastel rainbow swirled around them. Everything shimmered in light shades of blue, yellow, green, and pink. Rachel and Kirsty reached for each other's hand as their delicate wings unfolded.

"Listen," said Kirsty. "The rain sounds different."

"Yes, I can't hear the raindrops spattering against the window anymore,"

said Rachel. "It sounds more like . . . waves."

At that moment, the pastel-colored swirl of fairy dust vanished, and the girls found themselves sitting on a small stretch of golden sand.

"It *is* waves," said Kirsty in delight. "Yippee, we made it to the beach after all."

"This is a bit more magical than the one I was planning to visit," said Rachel with a happy laugh.

"Welcome to Mermicorn Island," said Evelyn.

"I've never seen such fine sand," said Kirsty, letting it run through her fingers.

"Or such blue sea," Rachel added, cartwheeling down to the shore.

The sun was sparkling on the water, and it looked as if tiny diamonds were dancing in the waves. As Rachel turned around to smile at her best friend, she saw a beautiful sight. At the edge of the beach was a row of candy-colored stalls gleaming with a pearly sheen. Fairies were walking barefoot from stall to stall, wearing shells braided into their hair and pearls threaded into necklaces and

belts. The Music Fairies were playing an oceanic tune on driftwood instruments.

"I can taste the salt in the air," said Kirsty, taking a deep breath.

"What happens at the Mermicorn Festival?" Rachel asked.

"Music, dancing, good food, good fun," said Evelyn, spinning around with her arms held wide. "It's my favorite time of year."

Just then, Shannon the Ocean Fairy came dancing across the sand toward them.

"Rachel and Kirsty!" she cried, giving them a hug. "It's great to see you. Evelyn, when will the mermicorns get here? I can't wait to see them."

"Very soon," said Evelyn. "Let's get everyone to come down to the shore."

"Why is everyone walking?" asked

Rachel as they watched their fairy
friends moving down to the shore.

"Because even fairies like to feel the
sand between our toes sometimes," said
Evelyn, smiling. "We all leave our wands
at the palace when we come here. We
agreed that Mermicorn Island should
only be for mermicorn magic."

Just then, the music changed. It was

as gentle and flowing as the waves.
The shallow, clear water began to swirl
around in a whirlpool.

"Wow, the water's changing color," said
Kirsty.

The whirlpool had turned a lighter,
more sparkling blue, and seemed to be lit
by a light from below.

"Something's coming out of it," said
Rachel, tingling all over with excitement.

Whirlpool Magic

Rachel and Kirsty watched as a spiral horn rose up through the swirling water. The head and neck of a beautiful unicorn appeared. Three colorful gemstones hung around her neck on a golden chain. Then a sparkling green mermaid tail flicked out of the water. The fairies

cheered and waved, and the mermicorn bowed its head. Evelyn waded out to the whirlpool and reached out her hand.

"This is Topaz," said Evelyn.

She let her hand rest on Topaz's mane for a moment. Rachel and Kirsty followed Evelyn and did the same thing, and at once a strong feeling of confidence flooded through them. At the

same time, the gems Topaz was wearing glowed even more brightly.

"How funny," said Kirsty. "I've been feeling worried about the homework project I chose to do for school, but all of a sudden I feel certain that I picked the right one."

Evelyn smiled.

"Topaz's magic is working," she said. "You see, the gems that she wears have the power to make everyone around them feel confident. Her blue gem gives you confidence in your own choices and ideas. Her pink gem gives you confidence to speak your mind, and helps you be brave enough to stand up for the things you believe in. And the green gem gives you the confidence to help others."

Just then, several other mermicorns

broke through the foaming waters, each
with a different-colored tail. The other
fairies were all in the water now, and
they started to play with the mermicorns,
stroking their manes, laughing, and
singing. The mermicorns were leaping
through the foamy waves, flicking their

tails. Topaz nuzzled close to Evelyn, with love in her big, shining eyes.

"What an amazing sight," said Rachel, looking around in wonder at the fairies and mermicorns.

"This festival gives us confidence and energy every year," said Evelyn. "And the mermicorns love spending time with the fairies. We've planned a feast on the beach for later and a dance under the moonlight. This is going to be the best festival yet."

"WRONG!" yelled a raspy voice.

There was a loud roar, and something came hurtling through the water toward the fairies and the mermicorns.

"A speedboat!" cried Rachel.

The boat turned hard in the waves, sending a wall of water crashing over

the fairies. There were three goblins
in the back of the boat, and everyone
recognized the driver.

"Jack Frost," said Kirsty. "We should

have guessed."

"Get her!" shouted Jack Frost.

Cackling with laughter, the goblins
threw an ice-blue net over Topaz.

"You can't catch a magical mermicorn

with a fishing net," said Evelyn, fluttering
her wings. "It can't hold her."

"This isn't an ordinary net," said Jack
Frost with a sneer. "Besides, it's not your
silly mermicorn I want. I heard a rumor
that her gems make you feel confident.
Now I know why you pesky fairies are
always thinking you know best. Without
the gems, you'll never be confident

enough to stand up to me!"

"Stop!" cried Kirsty. "You wouldn't dare take them when you're surrounded by fairies."

"Fairies without their wands," scoffed Jack Frost. "You can't stop me!"

He tugged on the net, and it snapped back into his hand. The little mermicorn let out a cry of shock. Then Jack Frost held up the three gems.

"My magical net catches whatever I

want," he gloated. "And I want these."

There was a flash of blue light and a crack of thunder, and the speedboat disappeared, taking Jack Frost and the magical gems with it.

All at Sea

The mermicorns gathered around
Topaz, looking frightened and unhappy.
Evelyn put her arms out to try to pet
them all.

"What are we going to do?" she asked.

Some of the other fairies made a circle
around the mermicorns.

"I think we should go and get our wands," said Shannon.

"First we should tell the king and queen what's happened," said Victoria the Violin Fairy.

They exchanged a worried glance.

"Maybe you're right," said Shannon in a shaky voice.

"No, maybe your idea is better," said Victoria.

Rachel and Kirsty looked around. All the fairies started talking at once, sharing their ideas. But no one felt sure which idea was best. At last, Evelyn rose out of the water and fluttered above everyone.

"It's hard to have the confidence to decide, because Topaz's gems are missing," she said. "We have to get them back."

"Maybe we should ask the king and queen what to do," said Shannon.

The fairies murmured and nodded, and then shrugged their shoulders and stared at one another. No one felt confident enough to make a choice.

Kirsty felt unsure, too. But then she remembered that her best friend always

made her feel stronger. She took Rachel's
hand, and a little bit of confidence
flickered inside her.

"Let me and Rachel try to rescue the
gems," she said.

"Not without me," said Evelyn.

"Should the rest of us go back to the
Fairyland Palace?" asked Victoria.

She didn't sound very sure, but Rachel and Kirsty nodded, and the fairies hugged them good-bye and flew away.

"Let's fly toward the Ice Castle," said Kirsty, still holding tightly to Rachel's hand. "Maybe we will have a better idea on the way."

Evelyn came over and the three friends held hands. Instantly they all felt a little bit more confident.

"Topaz, go home to Mermicorn City,"
said Evelyn. "You'll be safe there until we
can find your gems."

Topaz turned to the other mermicorns
and made a few gentle whinnying sounds.
At once, the mermicorns dove under the
waves with a flick of their bright tails. But
Topaz did not join them. She looked at
Evelyn and shook her head.

"She won't go home without her
gems," said Evelyn. "All right, Topaz,
I understand. Maybe you can help us
search."

Feeling unsure of where to start looking,
the fairies rose up and started to fly. Topaz
swam below them, leaping through the
waves. They had not gone far before the
mermicorn let out a high-pitched whinny
and speeded up.

"She's seen something," said Evelyn. "Come on!"

Topaz was already ahead of them. She was streaking through the water toward a little boat in the distance.

"Is that the speedboat?" asked Evelyn.

"No," said Kirsty. "It looks like a rowboat."

"There are two people in it," said Rachel in an excited voice. "I think they're green."

35

The three fairies reached the little red boat bobbing on the water and hovered above it. Sure enough, two grumpy-faced goblins were squatting inside.

"What should we do?" asked Evelyn. "I can't decide."

Topaz was swimming around the boat, and the goblins were yelling at her.

"Go away!"

"Leave us alone, you big goldfish!"

Rachel zoomed down and perched on the side of the boat. Kirsty and Evelyn landed beside her. At once, Topaz's velvety head rose out of the water. She was glaring at the bigger goblin, and Evelyn gasped.

"Look at his hand," she said.

The goblin had something clutched in his fist. He was trying to hide it, but a bright blue light was shining through his closed fingers.

"The blue gem," said Rachel. "We've found it!"

Topaz to the Rescue

"Give Topaz's gem back," said Kirsty.

But the goblin just blew a raspberry at her and dropped the gem back in his pocket.

"What are we going to do?" asked Evelyn. "I don't have my wand, so we can't use magic to help us."

Kirsty had an idea.

"Goblins, do you enjoy being out here on the boat by yourselves?" she asked.

The goblins shook their heads.

"It's boring," said one.

"I'm hungry," said the other.

"If you give us the gem, you'll be able to go home," said Kirsty. "You won't need to guard anything."

"We'd need to guard ourselves against Jack Frost," said the bigger goblin. "Go away and leave us alone."

He waved an arm at them and accidentally hit the smaller goblin in the face.

"Watch out," said the smaller goblin.

The bigger goblin poked his shoulder with one long, bony finger. The smaller goblin gave him a shove.

"Stop squabbling," said Rachel.

But the goblins took no notice. They stood up and jostled each other. The bigger goblin stamped on the smaller goblin's toes.

"YOWCH!" he yelled, hopping around on one leg.

He lost his balance and fell sideways. *SPLASH!* He sent the bigger goblin

straight over the side of the boat and into the water!

"Help!" gurgled the bigger goblin. "Help! I can't swim!"

Evelyn was about to help, but Kirsty stopped her.

"Wait," she said. "Look. Maybe this time, we need to give the mermicorn magic a chance."

Topaz dove under the goblin, and suddenly he was riding a mermicorn! A happy smile spread over his face. He leaned forward and pressed his face into Topaz's mane. He cuddled her and stroked her soft skin. Then he reached into his pocket and gave back the blue gem.

"Thank you for saving me," he whispered.

Rachel and Kirsty were astonished.

They had never seen a goblin be so
gentle.

"Perhaps it's the mermicorn magic,"
said Kirsty in a whisper. "It made me feel
wonderful when I stroked Topaz before.
Maybe it's making the goblin feel like
doing the right thing."

The goblin climbed back into the boat, and the fairies fluttered over to join Topaz. As the goblins rowed away, Topaz nuzzled each of the fairies. Evelyn threw her arms around Rachel and Kirsty.

"Thank you for being with me today," she said. "Without your help, I would never have found the blue gem."

"You're welcome," said Kirsty. "I just

hope that we can help you find the other gems soon."

"Me, too," said Evelyn. "Without them, people and fairies will lose their confidence."

"Let's go and get your wand back," said Kirsty. "Then we can start making a plan to find the other gems."

Rachel smiled at her.

"It's great to hear you sounding confident again," she said. "Race you to the Fairyland Palace!"

Evelyn did a spin and fluttered into the air. Kirsty and Rachel both cheered and then followed her.

Speaking Your Mind

Contents

Jack Frost's Magical Snowflake

The towers of the pink Fairyland Palace glimmered in the sunshine. Rachel, Kirsty, and Evelyn fluttered down and landed on the polished steps. At once, the doors were flung open. Bertram the frog footman bowed and smiled at them.

"Her Majesty Queen Titania is waiting

for you at the Seeing Pool," he said.

"Thanks, Bertram," said Rachel. "It's great to see you again!"

The fairies zoomed around the palace to the gardens. They swooped under an archway of roses and landed beside the sparkling Seeing Pool. They had been here many times before, but they had never seen so many fairies gathered around the shining water.

"It looks as if everyone from the festival is here," said Kirsty.

Queen Titania was standing among the fairies. Rachel, Kirsty, and Evelyn curtsied to her.

"I knew that you would come," she said.

"We got Topaz's blue gem back, thanks to Rachel and Kirsty," said Evelyn.

"But Jack Frost still has the other two gems," said Kirsty. "Without them, people and fairies are going to lose the confidence to speak their minds and help others."

"We must find the gems," Rachel said.

"Let's find out what the Seeing Pool

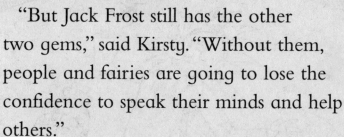

can tell us," said the queen.

She held her wand out over the water, and at once a picture appeared. It was as clear as a reflection in a mirror. Jack Frost was standing over a young goblin, clutching Topaz's pink gemstone in his hand.

"Take this to the goblin village and hide it," he said.

The goblin, who was wearing a knitted hat and sparkly orange sandals, snatched the gemstone. He threw it up into the air and caught it again, squawking with laughter.

"Do you think this is a joke?" snarled Jack Frost. "Those fairies will try all sorts of tricky things to get that gem."

"I'll hide it," the goblin promised, puffing out his chest. "Those sneaky fairies can't trick me."

"Of course they can," Jack Frost sneered. "But I'm going to give you

something that will stop them."

He pulled a small blue object from his cloak. It twinkled in the daylight, and the goblin gasped.

"I love it," he said. "What is it?"

"It's a magical snowflake," said Jack Frost. "If any fairies bother you, just

throw this at them. It'll turn into a net
and send them straight to the Ice Castle
dungeon."

"You're a genius," said the goblin,
staring at Jack Frost in awe.

Jack Frost threw back his spiky head
and cackled with delight. Then the
water of the Seeing Pool rippled, and the
picture faded away.

Queen Titania
turned to the fairies
with a serious
expression.

"With the
magical snowflake,
the goblin can send
any fairy to the
Ice Castle dungeon,"
she said. "It will be

dangerous and difficult to get the pink gemstone."

"I don't care how dangerous it is," said Evelyn. "Topaz and the other mermicorns are depending on me to help them. I'll go to the goblin village."

"We'll go with you," said Rachel at once. "Kirsty and I have been to Goblin Grotto before, and we might be able to help."

"Thank you," said Evelyn with a relieved smile.

Queen Titania handed Evelyn her wand. The other fairies clapped and called, "Good luck!" and "Be careful!" Then Rachel, Kirsty, and Evelyn curtsied to the queen and zoomed off into the blue sky. Glancing over her shoulder, Kirsty saw dozens of fairy wings glimmering and fluttering below. The queen's hand was raised as she waved good-bye.

"We can't let them down," Kirsty said fiercely. "We must get the gemstone and take it back to Topaz."

A Speech in Goblin Grotto

By the time the fairies reached Goblin
Grotto, the cold was making them shiver.
They landed in a narrow side street.
Cobbles poked through gray snow, dirty
from goblin feet. The street was lined
with the goblins' huts, and icicles hung
from the eaves.

"Time for a little mermicorn magic," said Evelyn, smiling.

She reached up and broke off the biggest icicle. As soon as her wand

touched it, the icicle started to shimmer like pearl, showing all the colors of the rainbow.

"It reminds me of Topaz's horn," said Rachel.

Evelyn tapped each of them on the
shoulder with the icicle. At once, they
stopped feeling cold.

"It's like wearing an invisible coat," said
Kirsty.

"The magic will last until the icicle
melts," said Evelyn.

She attached the icicle to the eaves

again and looked around. There wasn't a goblin in sight.

"Where shall we start looking?" she asked.

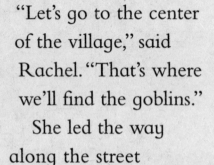

"Let's go to the center of the village," said Rachel. "That's where we'll find the goblins." She led the way along the street toward the square in the middle of the village. As they got closer, they heard someone shouting.

"What's that?" Evelyn whispered in a trembling voice.

They were close to the central square now. Carefully, they peeped around the corner. A goblin was standing on an upside-down wooden crate, surrounded

by a crowd of other goblins. They were staring at him with their mouths hanging open.

"And another thing!" he was shouting. "I'm not afraid to say that I like playing Guess That Goblin, even though some goblins think it's a children's game. Just because I'm young, that doesn't

mean I'm not smart. I've got amazing ideas and plans. Jack Frost knows how wonderful and smart I am. You're all going to be sorry for laughing at me for saying the moon is made of green cheese. I can prove it."

"He seems a bit confused," said Evelyn. "Even for a goblin."

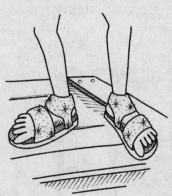

"Oh my goodness," said Rachel. "Look at his feet."

The loud young goblin was wearing sparkly orange sandals and a blue knitted hat.

"He must be the goblin that we saw in the Seeing Pool," said Kirsty. "He's got the pink gemstone."

"Of course," said Evelyn. "That's why he feels so confident in front of all these other goblins. The pink gemstone gives you the courage to speak your mind."

"We can't go up to him now," said Rachel. "All the goblins are staring at him."

But at that moment, the young goblin jumped down from his crate and stomped off down an alleyway.

"We have to follow him," Kirsty
whispered. "We'll just have to hope that
the other goblins don't see us."

Keeping their fingers crossed, the fairies
stayed in the shadows and fluttered along
the side of the square.

"There are his footprints," said Rachel,
pointing to a set of enormous goblin
prints in the snow. "They will lead us
right to him."

The fairies slipped into the tumble-down alleyway. They followed the prints until they reached a hut tucked in between two threadbare fir trees. It was hard to tell if the hut was as shabby as the alleyway, because it was covered in pictures. Rachel spotted several posters for Frosty and his Gobolicious Band. There were leaflets for goblin shops and even recipes with photographs of green-goo cupcakes and sludge sausages.

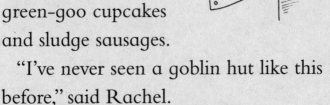

"I've never seen a goblin hut like this before," said Rachel.

"What now?" asked Kirsty. "As soon as the goblin spots us, he'll throw the magical snowflake."

"We have to get in without being seen," said Evelyn. "But how?"

Magical Mice

"There's no way we can get in," said
Rachel. "The huts are tiny inside. The
goblin would see us right away. Besides,
there's hardly enough room for a mouse
to creep in under the door, let alone a
fairy."

"Oh!" said Kirsty suddenly. "You've given me an idea. Evelyn, could you turn us into mice? If we were that small, we could creep in under the door."

"Yes, and we should be able to keep out of the goblin's sight," said Evelyn.

Just then, they heard goblin voices at the far end of the alleyway. "They're coming this way," said Rachel. "Hurry." Evelyn raised her wand and whispered a spell.

Ears and tail, small and light,
Good at keeping out of sight.
Change these fairies into mice;
We'll find the gemstone in a trice!

A wisp of sparkling fairy dust spiraled from her wand and rippled from Rachel to Kirsty and then back to Evelyn. As soon as it touched them, they felt fur

tickling their faces.

"My ears are getting bigger," said Kirsty with a giggle.

She reached up to touch them and realized that she had paws instead of hands.

"We're tiny," said Rachel, looking at Kirsty and Evelyn. They had all become

small, brown field mice.

"Those goblin voices are getting closer," said Evelyn.

Twitching their whiskers, the three mice scurried under the goblin's door and pressed themselves up against the wall of

the hut.

The young goblin was sitting in front of a feeble fire, rubbing his bony hands together. He had kicked off his orange sandals, but his hat was still perched on top of his knobbly head.

"No silly fairies are going to find my hiding place," he said, squawking with laughter. "I'll be the first goblin ever to beat the fairies and follow Jack Frost's orders. I'll be made chief goblin. I'll get medals. I'll make the others call me 'sir.'"

He reached out to a pile of green-goo cupcakes on a little table and shoved one

into his mouth.

"They'll never guess I've hidden it in my chimney," he said, spraying green crumbs across the floor. "And even if they do, they're not going to want to singe their little wings."

The mice exchanged worried glances.

"The goblin's right," Kirsty whispered. "We can't get into the chimney as mice or as fairies!"

Green-Goo Distraction

"I have an idea," said Rachel. "If the goblin thinks that we've guessed his hiding place, he might move the gemstone himself."

"And then we would have a chance to take it back," said Kirsty.

"We have to let him hear us," said
Evelyn.

Rachel and Kirsty looked at her in
surprise.

"Do you mean that you want us to get
caught?" Rachel asked.

"No," said Evelyn. "But what if the
goblin hears fairy voices talking about
his hiding place?"

Rachel and Kirsty ran around the edge
of the hut. Kirsty stopped by the fireplace
and Rachel scurried behind a large,
moldy marshmallow.

Evelyn put her paws over her mouth to
make it sound as if she was outside.

"He's in here," she called.

The goblin leaped to his feet and pulled
out the magical snowflake.

On the other side of the room, Rachel

said, "We have to get in. He can't catch us all with that magical snowflake."

"They can see me!" the goblin squeaked.

He raced to the door and bolted it shut. Then he ran to the window and shut the curtains.

"Let's fly down the chimney," said Kirsty. "That's a good hiding place."

"Oh, no you don't," muttered the goblin. "I'm smarter than you."

He sprang toward the fireplace and reached up inside the chimney. When he pulled his hand out, he was holding a small velvet pouch.

"I'll fool them," he whispered.

He dropped the pouch into a cracked glass jar on the mantelpiece. Then he sat down, but he didn't relax. He sat bolt upright, watching the chimney. Rachel and Kirsty ran back around the room to where Evelyn was waiting.

"We have to distract him," said Rachel. "If he sees a fairy, he'll use the magic snowflake."

Kirsty looked at the table where the

green-goo cupcakes were piled up. She smiled, and her whiskers bristled.

"The goblin wouldn't like two little mice nibbling his cakes," she said. "If we can keep him watching us, maybe Evelyn can turn back into a fairy and take the gemstone without him noticing."

"It's risky," said Rachel. "If he turns

around and sees her, he'll send her to the dungeon."

"We won't let him turn around," said Kirsty. "We'll be the strangest, most annoying mice he's ever seen. We just can't let him know that we're really fairies."

"Let's try," said Evelyn. "Let's do it for the mermicorns."

Back to the Ocean

Rachel and Kirsty scampered around to the back of the goblin's chair. The space between the floor and the chair was just big enough for them to squeeze through. It was dark and dusty under there. They crawled past snoozing spiders and stale cupcake crumbs.

"I see the goblin's legs," Rachel

whispered.

"Go left," said Kirsty. "The table's at the side of the chair."

Side by side, the two mice edged out from underneath the chair. They each chose a table leg.

"How do we climb up?" Kirsty asked.

"I think we just dig our tiny little claws in and use our tails to balance,"

 said Rachel, her whiskers twitching as she smiled. "I'm hoping it comes naturally."

Silently, they climbed up the table legs, going faster and faster. They reached the

top at the same time. A mountain of green cakes towered above them.

"Those cakes smell really bad," Rachel whispered.

"Let's each choose one," said Kirsty. "Then we just have to do everything we can to keep him looking at us."

They each pulled a cake toward them, and then Rachel let out a loud *SQUEAK!* The goblin turned to look at her.

"Hey, get off my cakes!" he yelled.

He swiped at the little mouse, but she dodged him and started nibbling.

Before he could try to hit her again,
Kirsty squeaked, too.

"Get out of here!" the goblin screeched.
He snatched at the mice, trying to

catch them, but they were too quick
for him. Kirsty and Rachel ran left and
right, leaping over his hand and even
swinging under the table with their tails.
"You squeaky little pests," he yelled.
"Come here!"

In between leaps and swings, Rachel
saw Evelyn fluttering in front of the
mantelpiece. But just
as she reached for
the jar, the goblin
started to turn
around.

SQUEAK!
The mice sprang
through the air
and landed on the
front of the goblin's
knitted hat. Clinging

on with their front paws, they jumped
down and pulled the hat over his eyes.

"Help!" the goblin shrieked. "Mouse
attack!"

He spun around, trying to swipe at the
dangling mice. Just as he snatched the hat
from his head, Evelyn grabbed the velvet
bag from the jar and waved her wand.

"Fairies!" the goblin shouted.

He flung the
magical snowflake
at Evelyn, just as
she and the mice
disappeared in a
twinkling of fairy
dust.

Rachel and
Kirsty blinked, and
saw that they were
fluttering above the
blue ocean.

"We're fairies again," said Rachel.
"Thank goodness."

Evelyn put her arms around them, and
all three of them twirled around in the air,
laughing. "That was close," Evelyn said.
"It's thanks to you that I'm safe, and that
I have this."

She took the pink gemstone out of the velvet pouch, and it seemed to glow more brightly.

"How will you tell Topaz that you've got it back?" Rachel asked.

"I think she already knows," said Evelyn. "She has a very special

connection with the gems."

She flew down and held the gem in the water. At once, the water began to whirl around, changing from blue to pink. The whirlpool spun faster and deeper. Then a spiral horn rose out of the water.

"Topaz!" cried all the fairies at once.

Evelyn placed the gem back in Topaz's necklace, and then they all put their

arms around the mermicorn's neck. She
nuzzled them gratefully.

"There's one more gem to find," said
Evelyn. "But before we go looking for it,
how about a swim with a mermicorn?"

Rachel and Kirsty exchanged an excited smile.

"Yes please!" they exclaimed.

Topaz whinnied and splashed in the waves. It looked like she was ready for a celebratory swim, too!

Helping Others

Contents

Return to
Mermicorn Island

Evelyn, Rachel, and Kirsty had fun
diving through the foaming waves with
Topaz, but they didn't play for long.
Jack Frost still had the green gemstone,
and without it none of the fairies would
have the confidence to help others. Soon,
the three friends were hurrying along a

marble hallway in the Fairyland Palace.

"I'm glad we can give the queen some good news," said Kirsty. "The last time we saw her, the pink gemstone was still missing."

They entered the throne room. Queen Titania was standing beside the window, gazing out over Fairyland. She turned when the fairies came in, and they curtsied. The queen looked worried.

"We found the pink gemstone," said Rachel. "Now there is just one left to find."

"Thank you," said the queen. "You have been very brave. I wish I knew what to tell you to do next. But now that Jack Frost has the green gemstone, I don't feel sure that my advice is wise."

"I'm sorry, Your Majesty," said Evelyn, hanging her head.

The queen came forward and placed one hand on Evelyn's shoulder.

"The only person to blame is Jack Frost," she said.

"Where are the fairies from the festival?" asked Kirsty, gazing around. The throne room was empty apart from Bertram the frog footman.

"They have gone back to Mermicorn Island," said the queen. "I am not sure why."

"Maybe we should go back to the island, too," said Rachel.

"Perhaps," said the queen. "I'm not sure. The only thing I know is that I won't be able to give advice until the green gemstone is back where it belongs."

The fairies curtsied and turned to leave. At the throne room door, Bertram spoke shyly to them.

"Excuse me," he said. "I think I know why the fairies went back to the island. It was because of the Amazing Advisor."

"Who's that?" asked Evelyn.

"All I know is that the Amazing Advisor told them everything would be all right if they went back to the island," he said. "He sounded very sure of himself and he gave great advice."

Rachel and Kirsty exchanged a puzzled glance.

"Who could he be?" Kirsty asked.

"I don't know," Rachel replied. "But I
think we should go right to Mermicorn
Island and find out."

The fairies flew out across the shining
blue sea. The tall, slender trees of
Mermicorn Island were bending in the
warm, gentle breeze.

"The island looks like a green gemstone in the water," said Kirsty.

The fairies on the golden beach were lining up outside a blue tent. It was decorated with white shells, and the sign beside it said:

The Amazing Advisor's Seashell Cave
FREE Advice for Fairies

There were so many fairies crowding around the entrance that it was impossible to see inside.

"Let's look around the back," Rachel suggested. "Maybe we can find a clue."

They fluttered around and saw that there was a small flap on the other side of the tent.

"It's just like a back door," said Evelyn.

At that moment, the flap was lifted and two figures stepped out of the tent. They were wearing long blue capes that reached the ground, with huge hoods that covered their faces. Each of them was wearing a badge that said *Amazing Advisor's Helper*. The capes were decorated with the same white shells as the tent.

They sat down on two driftwood logs. One of the helpers pulled a green bottle from under his cape. He twisted the lid and fizzy green bubbles spurted out.

"Yum!" said the other helper, snatching the bottle and taking a big glug. "I love cabbage soda."

"What a squawky voice he has," said Kirsty.

The first helper burped and they both cackled with laughter.

"And what bad manners," said Evelyn.

"It's too hot on this island," grumbled the first helper. "And I'm fed up with fairies."

He threw back his hood, and Rachel clutched Kirsty's hand.

"Oh no," said Evelyn. "Goblins!"

The Amazing Advisor

The three fairies darted out of sight
behind the sand dunes. They peered out
from behind a clump of beach grass. The
second goblin was busy complaining.

"Why can't we go home?" he whined.
"I'm worried that all the goodness and
sweetness here is contagious."

"I'm sure I'm allergic to fairy dust," said the first goblin. "But we can't go home until that mermicorn turns up. Jack Frost won't stop yelling at us until he has her gemstones back."

The three fairies exchanged worried glances.

"Come on," said the second goblin, finishing the last drops of cabbage soda. "Maybe the mermicorn will turn up soon. Then we can jump in the boat, catch it, and get back to Goblin Grotto."

Putting their hoods up again, they ducked back into the tent.

"So they've got a boat," said Rachel. "They're planning to catch Topaz."

Evelyn gave a little sniff, and tears glistened in her eyes.

"Don't worry," said Kirsty, putting her

arm around Evelyn and giving her a
squeeze. "We won't let them take Topaz.
We're one step ahead of them already,
because we know their plan. We have to
warn the other fairies."

"Let's just see if we can hear anything
else," said Rachel.

They fluttered closer and pressed their
ears against the tent. At once they heard
a strange, deep voice.

"How can I help you, young fairy?"

"That must be the Amazing Advisor," Kirsty whispered. "I suppose it's another goblin in disguise."

"I want to protect my magical objects from Jack Frost," said a clear, musical voice. "What should I do?"

"Hide them under a potted plant in your garden," boomed the Amazing Advisor. "Next!"

Another fairy voice spoke. "I feel as if all my confidence has been taken away. How can I be the best that I can be?"

"Easy," said the Amazing Advisor. "Confidence isn't about being the best you that you can be. It's about being better than other people. Have a competition with your friends that you know you can win. Next!"

"The Amazing Advisor doesn't sound
very amazing to me," said Rachel. "What
awful advice!"

"But he sounds so confident that the
fairies are listening to him," said Kirsty,
groaning.

"He must have the green gemstone,"
said Evelyn. "It's giving him the
confidence to advise others."

"The Amazing Advisor is taking a break," squawked one of the goblin advisors. "Come back later."

The back flap of the tent trembled, and the fairies darted out of sight. A tall figure in a bright-blue cloak stepped out of the tent, followed by four goblin helpers. He threw back his hood, and the fairies gasped. The Amazing Advisor wasn't another goblin after all. It was Jack Frost himself!

Going Fishing

"Give me some water," Jack Frost
snapped at the goblins. "Using that deep
voice is hurting my throat."

While the goblins scurried to obey, Jack
Frost touched the green gemstone that

hung around his neck under his cloak.

"The last gemstone," whispered Evelyn.

"From now on, no one can feel better or more important than me," said Jack Frost with a thin smile. "The fairies won't be able to advise anyone, and I'll take over in the confusion. Fairyland will be mine!"

He threw his head back and cackled with laughter.

"I want to go home," whined the tallest goblin.

Jack Frost stopped cackling and turned on him with blazing eyes.

"Go and eavesdrop

on the fairies," he yelled. "They're bound to spot the mermicorn as soon as it turns up. Then we'll show it this gemstone and it'll follow us anywhere. Go!"

The goblin scurried back into the tent.

"Soon all the mermicorn magic will belong to me," said Jack Frost. "I've heard mermicorns can time-travel, grant wishes, and cure illness."

"Those are just legends," Evelyn muttered. "Topaz can't do those things. But if Jack Frost gets the gemstones again, he will be more powerful than ever."

"He'll be mad when he finds out that Topaz can't do what he wants," said Kirsty.

"We have to stop him," said Rachel. "Luckily the island is full of fairies. Let's go and tell them who the Amazing

Advisor really is."

But before they could move, the tallest goblin came tumbling out of the tent.

"It's back!" he squealed. "One of the fairies said she saw a horn in the water."

"At last!" said Jack Frost, throwing off his cloak. "The boat is on the other side of the island. Go!"

The goblins sprinted off and Jack Frost disappeared in a flash of blue lightning.

"There's no time to tell the other fairies," said Evelyn. "We have to save Topaz!"

Rachel, Kirsty, and Evelyn zoomed across the island. They flew over the goblins below and soon reached the other side of the island. A little ice-blue fishing trawler was bobbing on the water. Jack Frost was in the cabin.

"Let's hide behind the boat," said Kirsty. "The goblins will be here any minute."

They ducked down at the back of the boat just in time. The goblins burst out of a clump of trees and clambered on board.

"Get this boat moving!" Jack Frost roared. "Go around to where the mermicorn was seen. Faster!"

Soon the boat was chugging around the island. The fairies clung on to the back, keeping their heads down.

"We have to get the gemstone back before Topaz sees it," said Evelyn. "Otherwise I won't be able to stop her from following the boat."

They peeked over the side and saw Jack Frost put the gemstone in a bottle and cork it up. He tied one end of a rope around the bottle. Then he threw the bottle over the back of the boat and dragged it along behind them, holding on to the rope.

"Now all we have to

do is wait for the mermicorn to spot it," he said. "When the mermicorn follows it, we'll lead it into deeper water and capture it—and all its other magical gemstones, too."

Magical Bubbles

The fairies exchanged worried glances.

"We can't go and untie the rope with Jack Frost watching," said Kirsty.

"We'd be spotted at once if we flew over and pulled the bottle out of the water," said Evelyn.

"We have to get to the bottle from underneath," said Rachel. "That's the

only way to reach it without being spotted. Then we can uncork the bottle and save the gemstone."

"But we can't swim underwater for long without coming up for air, and the boat is really fast," said Evelyn. "Jack Frost will see us."

The boat chugged along, and spray flew into the fairies' eyes. Suddenly, Kirsty had an idea.

"Rachel, do you remember our adventure with Shannon the Ocean Fairy?" she asked. "If Evelyn could put magical bubbles on our heads, we could breathe underwater."

"Yes, I know Shannon's bubbles spell," said Evelyn. "I can do it, but my magic works differently from hers. The bubbles won't be strong enough for you to dive very deep. You will have to stay near the surface."

"That's OK," said Rachel. "We don't need to dive down far to get the bottle."

Each of them took a deep breath and dove underwater. Three shiny bubbles floated out of Evelyn's wand and settled over their heads.

"We can breathe," said Rachel.

"But the boat is getting away," said
Kirsty.

Evelyn pointed her wand at the water
behind them, and it started to bubble
and churn. Then, *WHOOSH!* The water
pushed them forward until they were just
below the bottle.

"I've got it!" cried Rachel, slipping the
bottle out of the rope.

But in her excitement, she lifted her
head and it broke the surface of the
water. Jack Frost spotted her at once.

"Fairies!" he shrieked. "Goblins, get
them!"

The engine stopped and there were four
splashes as the goblins belly flopped into
the water.

"Uncork it!" cried Kirsty.

But a bony green hand wrenched the bottle away from Rachel. The goblin cackled and rattled the gemstone under Rachel's nose.

"Give it back," said Kirsty. "It doesn't belong to you."

"It does now," said the goblin, making a face at her.

He threw the bottle to another goblin,

but Evelyn rose out of the water and caught it. The third goblin snatched at her wings and pulled her backward, and the bottle flew out of her hand.

"Butterfingers," squawked the fourth goblin. "Hey, watch this!"

He balanced the bottle on his head. At that moment, a whirlpool of color appeared behind him. A spiral horn broke through the water.

"Topaz!" cried Kirsty in delight.

Topaz whinnied loudly and made the goblin jump. The precious bottle fell off his head . . . and sank beneath the waves. "The gemstone!" cried Evelyn.

Pearl's Present

"No!" Jack Frost roared.

Rachel and Kirsty dove after the bottle. It was already far below, turning over and over as it sank. They tried to follow it, but there was a loud *POP* and their bubbles burst. Holding their breath, they swam back to the surface. Below,

the green gemstone disappeared into the darkness.

When Rachel and Kirsty reached the surface, the goblins were clambering back onto the boat.

"You silly goblins!" Jack Frost was

yelling at them. "Fuzz for brains! Get this boat moving and don't you dare drip on me!"

He whirled around and glared at Topaz and the fairies. They treaded water, staring up at him.

"At least you've lost the gemstone, too," he hissed. "No fairy will ever feel confident about helping anyone again."

The trawler chugged away toward the shore. The roar of the engine faded.

"I'm so sorry, Evelyn," said Rachel, turning to the Mermicorn Fairy with tears in her eyes. "We've let you down."

"It wasn't your fault," said Evelyn. "Oh, Topaz, I'm sorry."

The mermicorn hung her head and the fairies wrapped their arms around her.

SPLASH!

A large, silvery tail had risen out of the
water. Rainbow colors danced across it.
With another splash, the tail disappeared.
Then a head rose out of the water. Blue
eyes twinkled at them, and long blond
hair fanned out upon the waves.

"It's a mermaid," said Rachel in a
whispery voice.

The mermaid smiled.

"My name is Pearl," she said. "I couldn't resist meeting the only two humans who have traveled to Fairyland."

"It's incredible to meet you," said Kirsty.

"I was just waiting for Jack Frost to leave before I gave you this," Pearl said to Evelyn. "It landed beside me as I was pruning the seaweed."

She lifted her hand out of the water, holding the precious bottle. The green gemstone glowed inside it. Evelyn let out a cry of delight. In a moment, the gemstone was out of the bottle and back around Topaz's neck.

"Thank you, Pearl,"

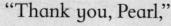

said Kirsty. "You've saved the day!"

Pearl smiled again. Then, with a flick of her shining tail, she was gone.

"I can't wait to tell the others the good news," said Evelyn. "Rachel and Kirsty, how can I ever thank you? Without you there would be no Mermicorn Festival and no confident fairies."

"It really was a wonderful watery adventure," said Rachel.

Evelyn hugged them both, and Topaz dipped her horn into the water. The waves changed color around them, shifting between all the colors of the rainbow.

"That's her way of saying 'thank you,'" said Evelyn.

Rachel and Kirsty buried their faces in the mermicorn's beautiful mane. It

was soft and warm, and it smelled like
jasmine. Suddenly, everything started to
spin around. Laughing and dizzy, the girls
looked up and saw that they were back
in Rachel's living room. The fire was
crackling in the grate, and the rain was
still beating on the window.

"Here we are," said Mr. Walker, coming
in with a tray. "Two hot chocolates with

whipped cream and sprinkles."

Rachel and Kirsty shared a happy smile. As usual, no time had passed while they had been away.

"That's one of the things I love about Fairyland," said Kirsty. "Even after the most incredible adventure, there's still a whole week of vacation ahead of us."

"As well as two mugs of the best hot chocolate in the world," said Rachel. "Yum!"

The two friends clinked their mugs in a toast. "To Fairyland!" they cheered together.

Rachel and Kirsty have found Evelyn's
missing magic gemstones. Now it's time
for them to help

Alicia
the Snow Queen Fairy!

Join their adventure in this
special sneak peek…

Dull December

"What an icy, gray December this is," said Rachel Walker, blowing on her fingers and shivering. "I'm starting to wonder if it will ever be Christmas!"

It was Saturday morning, and Rachel was in her backyard with her best friend, Kirsty Tate. They had come out to play a game of ball, but sleet was coming down. Kirsty shivered, too, and buried her hands deep into her pockets.

"I'm really glad I'm staying with you for the weekend, but I wish the weather wasn't so horrible," Kirsty said.

"We had such awesome plans," said Rachel. "But nature walks and boating on the lake won't be much fun when it's so miserable and freezing. It looks as if we'll be spending most of the weekend inside."

"Never mind," said Kirsty, smiling at her friend. "We always have fun when we're together, no matter what we're doing."

"You're right," said Rachel, trying to forget about the dark clouds above.

"Let's go inside," Kirsty said. "I think it's starting to snow."

"Oh, really?" said Rachel, feeling more cheerful. "Maybe we can go sledding."

"I don't think so," said Kirsty. "I only see one snowflake."

She pointed up to the single, perfect snowflake. It was spiraling down from the gray sky. The girls watched it land on the edge of a stone birdbath.

"That's funny," said Rachel after a moment. "It's not melting."

Kirsty took a step closer to the birdbath. "I think it's getting bigger," she said.

The snowflake began to grow bigger and bigger. Then it popped like a snowy balloon, and the girls saw a tiny fairy standing in its place. She was as exquisite as the snowflake had been. Her blond hair flowed around her shoulders, and she was wearing a long blue gown, decorated with sparkling silver sequins.

A furry cape
was wrapped
around her
shoulders, and
a snowflake
tiara twinkled
on her head.

"Hello, Rachel
and Kirsty," said
the fairy. "I'm
Alicia the Snow
Queen Fairy."

"Hello, Alicia!" said
Rachel. "It's great to meet you!"

"What are you doing here in
Tippington?" Kirsty asked.

"I've come to ask for your help," said
Alicia in a silvery voice. "It's my job to
make sure that everyone stays happy in

winter—in both the human and fairy
worlds. I went to visit Queen Titania
this morning, and when I came home
I got a terrible shock. Jack Frost had
gone into my home and taken my three
magical objects. Without the magical
snowflake, the enchanted
mirror, and the
everlasting
rose, I can't
look after
human
beings or
fairies this
winter."

"Oh
no, that's
awful!"
Rachel

exclaimed. "Is there any way that we can help you?"

Alicia clasped her hands together. "Please, would you come to Fairyland with me?" she asked. "Queen Titania has told me so much about you. When I discovered that my objects were missing, I thought of you right away. Will you help me find out what Jack Frost has done with them?"

Kirsty and Rachel nodded at once.

"Of course we will," Kirsty replied.

"Then let's go!" exclaimed Alicia, holding up her wand.

The Magical Tower

Glittering snowflakes burst from Alicia's
wand like a fountain and landed on
the girls.

"They're as light as butterfly kisses,"
said Rachel, laughing.

She and Kirsty had already shrunk to
fairy size, and their glittery wings were
fluttering, eager to fly. They felt a cool

wind whirl around them, lifting them into the air. They were carried up toward the dark clouds with Alicia at their side.

"I think the world's getting even more gloomy," said Kirsty, looking down.

Sleet was driving down all over Tippington, and the girls were glad to be leaving the bad weather behind. Better yet, they were going to Fairyland!

Rachel and Kirsty were secret friends with the fairies, and they always adored the magical adventures they shared.

Swirling snowflakes surrounded them now, until all they could see was glitter. When the snowflakes cleared, they were standing beside a tall white tower, and they were wrapped in warm fluffy capes, just like the one Alicia was wearing. All around, as far as they could see, were tall blue mountains, topped with snow.

"Welcome to my home," said Alicia, smiling at the girls.

The tower walls were not solid like the walls of the Fairyland Palace. Standing close to them, Rachel and Kirsty saw that they were made of swirling snow.

"That's amazing," said Rachel.

She reached out to touch the wall. It felt cold and coarse.

"But where's the door?" Kirsty asked.

"There is no door," said Alicia with a laugh. "You just need to trust me."

She took their hands and led them forward.

"We're going to walk into the wall!" Rachel exclaimed.

But she remembered what Alicia had said, and she kept walking. Instead of hitting the wall, they all walked straight through it and into Alicia's home!

It was warm and welcoming, with thick rugs, a roaring fire, and big sofas covered in cozy, colorful throw blankets. Hundreds of tiny golden lights hung around the room in graceful loops. When

the girls looked up, they saw that the
walls of the tower were covered with
twinkling lights all the way to the roof.

"Why doesn't the fire melt the tower?"
Kirsty asked.

"It's a magical fire," Alicia replied. "I

know spells to make it easy to live in cold weather. I have lived here for a long time, you see."

"Where are we?" asked Rachel.

"We are in the most remote part of Fairyland," said Alicia. "I live among the Blue Ice Mountains, far beyond Jack Frost's castle. He had no idea that I even lived here until this morning. His goblins drove his carriage the wrong way, and he arrived here while I was at the palace. I knew it was him because I saw goblin footprints in the snow. So he has my magical objects, and now both Fairyland and the human world are in danger."

"What do your magical objects do?" Kirsty asked.

Alicia waved her wand, and three pictures appeared in the air in front of the girls—a snowflake, a mirror, and a rose.

"The magical snowflake makes winter weather just right," she said. " The enchanted mirror helps everyone to see

the difference between good and bad.
The everlasting rose ensures that new life
is still growing underground, and that
flowers will appear again each spring.
Without them, winter will be miserable
for everyone, and my home will start to
suffer, just like the rest of Fairyland."

With another wave of her wand, the
pictures broke into tiny pieces and melted
away to nothing.

"What do you
mean?" asked
Rachel.

"Come with me
and I will show
you," said Alicia.

She flew upward,
and they followed
her, higher and

higher, until they passed through the roof
and fluttered up into the snow clouds
above.

"It's like flying through fluffy balls of
cotton," said Kirsty with a giggle.

Alicia led the way, and the girls sped
after her. Suddenly, there was a break in
the clouds, and they saw that Jack Frost's
Ice Castle was directly below them.
They were flying in the direction of the
Fairyland Palace!

SPECIAL EDITION

Which Magical Fairies Have You Met?

- ❏ Joy the Summer Vacation Fairy
- ❏ Holly the Christmas Fairy
- ❏ Kylie the Carnival Fairy
- ❏ Stella the Star Fairy
- ❏ Shannon the Ocean Fairy
- ❏ Trixie the Halloween Fairy
- ❏ Gabriella the Snow Kingdom Fairy
- ❏ Juliet the Valentine Fairy
- ❏ Mia the Bridesmaid Fairy
- ❏ Flora the Dress-Up Fairy
- ❏ Paige the Christmas Play Fairy
- ❏ Emma the Easter Fairy
- ❏ Cara the Camp Fairy
- ❏ Destiny the Rock Star Fairy
- ❏ Belle the Birthday Fairy
- ❏ Olympia the Games Fairy
- ❏ Selena the Sleepover Fairy

- ❏ Cheryl the Christmas Tree Fairy
- ❏ Florence the Friendship Fairy
- ❏ Lindsay the Luck Fairy
- ❏ Brianna the Tooth Fairy
- ❏ Autumn the Falling Leaves Fairy
- ❏ Keira the Movie Star Fairy
- ❏ Addison the April Fool's Day Fairy
- ❏ Bailey the Babysitter Fairy
- ❏ Natalie the Christmas Stocking Fairy
- ❏ Lila and Myla the Twins Fairies
- ❏ Chelsea the Congratulations Fairy
- ❏ Carly the School Fairy
- ❏ Angelica the Angel Fairy
- ❏ Blossom the Flower Girl Fairy
- ❏ Skyler the Fireworks Fairy
- ❏ Giselle the Christmas Ballet Fairy
- ❏ Alicia the Snow Queen Fairy

SCHOLASTIC

Find all of your favorite fairy friends at
scholastic.com/rainbowmagic

3 stories in each one!

HIT entertainment

RMSPECIAL20

RAINBOW magic

Which Magical Fairies Have You Met?

- ☐ The Rainbow Fairies
- ☐ The Weather Fairies
- ☐ The Jewel Fairies
- ☐ The Pet Fairies
- ☐ The Sports Fairies
- ☐ The Ocean Fairies
- ☐ The Princess Fairies
- ☐ The Superstar Fairies
- ☐ The Fashion Fairies
- ☐ The Sugar & Spice Fairies
- ☐ The Earth Fairies
- ☐ The Magical Crafts Fairies
- ☐ The Baby Animal Rescue Fairies
- ☐ The Fairy Tale Fairies
- ☐ The School Day Fairies
- ☐ The Storybook Fairies
- ☐ The Friendship Fairies

SCHOLASTIC

31901064468533

HIT entertainment

RMFAIRY17